Contents

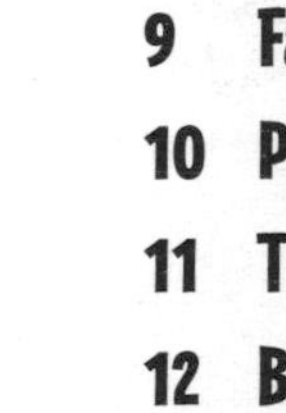
MANUAL of MISCHIEF!
TOP SECRET

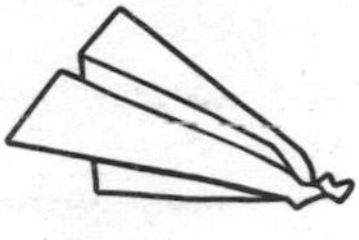

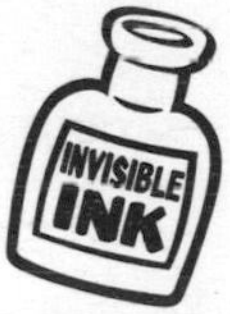
INVISIBLE INK

Welcome to...
BEANOTOWN!

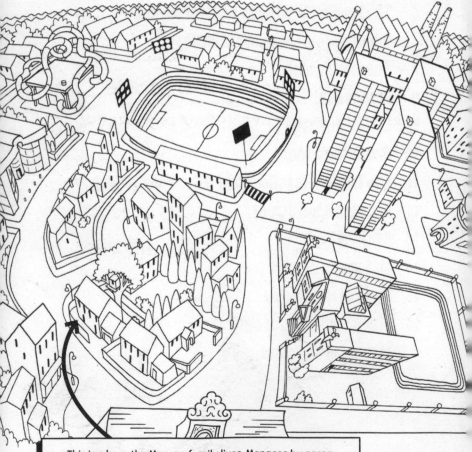

This is where the Menace family lives. Menaces by name,
Menaces by nature. At least that's what the neighbours say!

BEANO®
DENNIS & GNASHER
THE BATTLE FOR BASH STREET SCHOOL

I. P. DALEY
Craig Graham   Mike Stirling

Illustrated by
Nigel Parkinson

70004282207X

Farshore

First published in Great Britain 2021 by Farshore
An imprint of HarperCollins*Publishers*
1 London Bridge Street, London, SE1 9GF
www.farshore.co.uk

HarperCollins*Publishers*
1st Floor, Watermarque Building, Ringsend Road
Dublin 4, Ireland

Written by I.P Daley, Craig Graham & Mike Stirling
Edited by Thomas McBrien
Illustrated by Nigel Parkinson
Cover Design & Additional Illustration – Ed Stockham
Creative Services Manager – Usha Chauhan
Executive Producer – Rob Glenny
Art direction by Catherine Ellis
Text design by Janene Spencer

FUN STUFF THIS WAY

BEANO.COM

A Beano Studios Product © DC Thomson Ltd (2021)

ISBN 978 0 7555 0323 0
Printed in Great Britain
002

Farshore takes its responsibility to the planet and its inhabitants very seriously.
We aim to use papers from well-managed forests run by responsible suppliers.

MIX
Paper from
responsible sources
FSC™ C007454
FSC
www.fsc.org

This book is produced from independently certified FSC™ paper
to ensure responsible forest management.

For more information visit: www.harpercollins.co.uk/green

Chapter One

BREAKFAST AT DENNIS'S

You've probably never been to Beanotown, but it takes less than an hour to get here from wherever you live, as long as you travel by skateboard.

The 'Menace residence' (that's what Dad likes to say when he answers the phone) is the one with the tree house in the garden. That's where Dennis Menace lives.

Here he comes now . . .

Dennis hates doing anything the easy way. It keeps him on his toes, he says. Except this time, when it was keeping him on his fingers.

Dennis's awesome dog Gnasher followed him, yawning. It was breakfast time and Gnasher had done the doggy maths.

Breakfast = possible sausages = WIN!

That's not doggy maths – it's just maths.

Dennis pushed himself up with his hands, and landed with his butt* on the banister. He slid down the rail, making sure to grin awesomely. You never know when someone might video you and make you an online sensation.

The grin turned into a worried frown when his shorts started to heat up and he could feel his butt burning.

Stylin' it out!

OOH! HOT! HOT!

*They let me write 'butt' in a real book! I'm a legend...

Luckily, he was almost at the bottom when the first puffs of smoke appeared.

He leaped off the banister and flipped into the kitchen, somersaulting over the breakfast table and into an empty seat.

Dennis's mum, dad and baby sister Bea were already at the table.

'Morning, Dennis,' said Mum, barely batting an eyelid at her son's spectacular arrival. 'You're up early.'

'Mission accomplished!' said Dennis, high-fiving Bea, who giggled. Bea loved Dennis. Life was never dull when her big bro was around!

The toaster popped, firing two slices of toast into the air. In Beanotown, toasters actually launch toast way up into the air, just

4

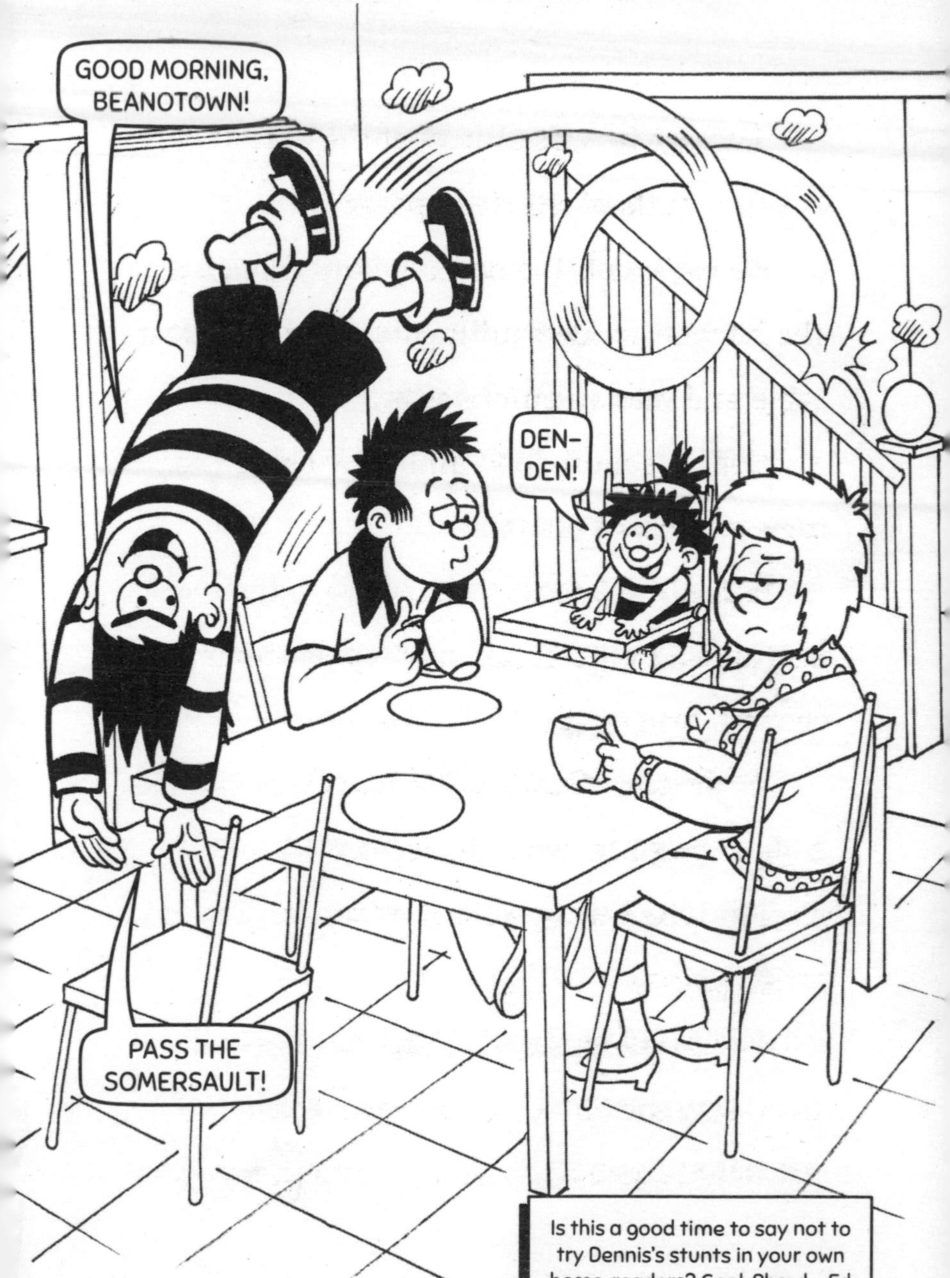
GOOD MORNING, BEANOTOWN!
DEN-DEN!
PASS THE SOMERSAULT!
Is this a good time to say not to try Dennis's stunts in your own home, readers? Cool. Phew! – Ed

like they should. Dennis grabbed the slices
before Dad could say, 'Hey, they're mine!'
He buttered and jammed the toast, slipping
one slice under the table for Gnasher.
It's gnot a sausage, Gnasher
thought, **but gnever mind**.

'What mission?' asked Dad,
putting some more bread in the toaster.

'From bed to breakfast without my
feet touching the floor,' said Dennis. '**Obvs.**'

Mum sighed. 'How many times have I told
you not to walk downstairs on your hands?'

'I didn't,' said Dennis, truthfully.

'There's something wrong with that
toaster,' said Dad, sniffing the air like Gnasher
does whenever he gets within two miles of a
butcher's shop.

'Sorry,' said Dennis, waving away the

final wisps of smoke rising from his overheated

shorts. 'That's me.'

Through mouthfuls of toast with butter and his favourite 'Blow a Raspberry' jam, Dennis told Mum and Dad about his plans for the day.

'I'm going to play hide-and-seek with the sharks at Beanotown Aquarium. Then I'm going blindfold hang-gliding. If I eat lunch while I'm in the air, I'll have time to dig for Greenbeard's pirate treasure at the beach before the tide comes in. Then . . .'

'But Dennis,' Mum interrupted. 'You're going back to school today . . . the summer holidays are . . .

....OVER!'

Numskulls are the little people who live in your head – everybody's got them!

This is what it's like in Dennis's head when the holidays are over . . .

*Funskulls are the happiest Numskulls! They're my faves, apart from the Bumskulls, that is . . .

'**WHAT?**' cried Dennis.

'But I've only been off for a day or two –
three, tops.'

'You've been off for seven weeks,' said
Mum. 'And you've already done all those
things this summer.'

'What use is a once-in-a-lifetime
experience if you can't ever do it again?'
Dennis grumped. 'Once-in-a-lifetime
experiences should be the rubbish stuff,
like tidying your room or emptying the
dishwasher.'

Dennis gloomily finished his toast then
stomped back to bed. **NO WAY** was he
getting up early on a school day!

Two hours later, Minnie, Rubi and Mandi were waiting for Dennis at the garden gate.

Minnie and Dennis are cousins, but you'd never know it.

Sure, they both loved jokes and adventures, and hated all rules, but Dennis always wore a red jumper with black stripes and Minnie always wore a black jersey with red stripes.

See? They couldn't be more different.

'Hi, cuz,' Minnie said, when Dennis finally stepped out of the house. 'Back to school already. Feels like the holidays only lasted a couple of days. Three, tops.'

'It could be worse, guys,' said Mandi.

'Oh yeah? What could be worse than going back to school?' asked Dennis.

If anyone knew how it could be worse, it was Mandi. She was a worrier, and spent a lot of time planning for what might happen. She once made a flow chart to find out what she should do if a llama attacked her with a loofah.

Now she isn't scared of llamas at all.
Loofahs still freaked her out a bit, but she
could live with that.

Rubi blew Dennis a big comedy kiss.
'For a start, all your mates go to Bash Street,'
she said. 'Like me!

MWAH!'

Rubi is super-smart
and has a wicked sense
of humour. She loves to
embarrass people.

'You **somehow**
get away with sneaking Gnasher
into class pretending he's your rucksack!' said
Minnie as Gnasher leapt onto Dennis's back.
He did a pretty good imitation of a rucksack.

'I know what would be worse,' said Mandi.
'Imagine . . . if you had to go to Beanotown
Academy?'

Beanotown Academy was the most admired school in Beanotown. It was always at the top of school league tables and its trophy cabinet groaned with shiny silver trophies and awards. Meanwhile, Bash Street School had come last in the league table for nine of the past ten years*, and all its trophy cabinet groaned with was despair.

'Ugh!' said Dennis. 'I heard the pupils have to salute the teachers.'

'And bow to the head!' said Minnie, rolling her eyes.

'They have to sing the school song every morning,' added Mandi.

---

* Bash Street would have come last every year if Miss Scooper's Finishing School for Perfect Pooches hadn't been included by accident one year. The dogs did okay in maths, science and English, but lost a lot of points for pooping in the playground, which hardly ever happens at Bash Street.

'Enough!' laughed Dennis. 'You've proved
your point – things COULD be worse!'

'Hello, losers,' said a sneering voice behind them.

'And now they ARE worse!' groaned Dennis, not looking round.

UH-OH!

IT'S WALTER!

Chapter Two

SKOOL DAZE

According to Walter Brown, Walter Brown is one of the most important people in Beanotown.

According to Dennis, he's the most annoying.

Walter never stops boasting about his rich and powerful family. His dad is Wilbur Brown, the mayor of Beanotown and the owner of WilburCorp, Beanotown's biggest, most evil* company.

* If WilburCorp's lawyers are reading this, then 'evil' is a typing mistake. It should be 'vile'. Thank you for not suing us!

'My father is visiting the school today,' said
Walter. 'He's got some *Big News*. You won't
like it.'

'Did you hear something?' Dennis asked Rubi.

'Just an annoying squeak,' said Rubi. 'Maybe I need to oil my wheels?'

'I hate you all,' huffed Walter, sticking his nose in the air. 'Just wait till you hear what my father has to say – then you won't be laughing!'

'That's true,' said Dennis, watching as Walter stomped off. 'His dad's the unfunniest man in the world. I wonder what the **Big News** is? It won't be anything good, I bet.'

As they walked through the gates of Bash Street School, Filbert Frogg stared down at them. He couldn't help it, because he was a statue. With a traffic cone on his head. Dennis had put it there last term.

LAUGH
-O-
METER

UNCONTROLLABLE
GUFFAW!!

ROFL-COPTER!

HA-HA!

LOL

ERM...

Bash Street School is a bit like an iceberg, and not just because the heating doesn't work. No, just like an iceberg, most of Bash Street

Gloria the gargoyle

Donald Dripp, Bash Street School's 2nd head teacher

Caused by Dennis

School is hidden from view.

This is what you can see from the road outside . . .

School clock. Runs fast at break, slow in class!

Greg the gar . . . boy?

Filbert Frogg, Bash Street School's 1st head teacher

Caused by Dennis

Caused by . . . you guessed it!

But this is what's actually there!

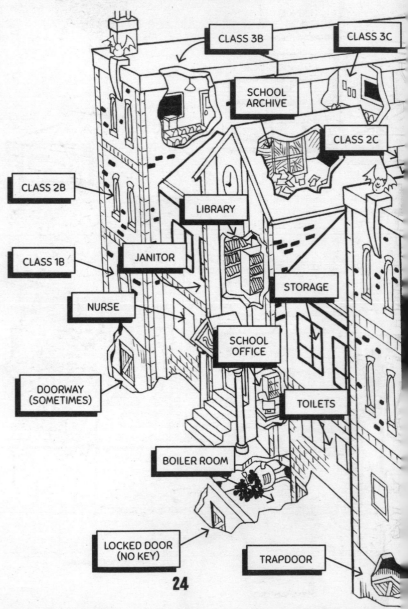

CLASS 3B
CLASS 3C
SCHOOL ARCHIVE
CLASS 2C
CLASS 2B
LIBRARY
CLASS 1B
JANITOR
STORAGE
NURSE
SCHOOL OFFICE
DOORWAY (SOMETIMES)
TOILETS
BOILER ROOM
LOCKED DOOR (NO KEY)
TRAPDOOR

24

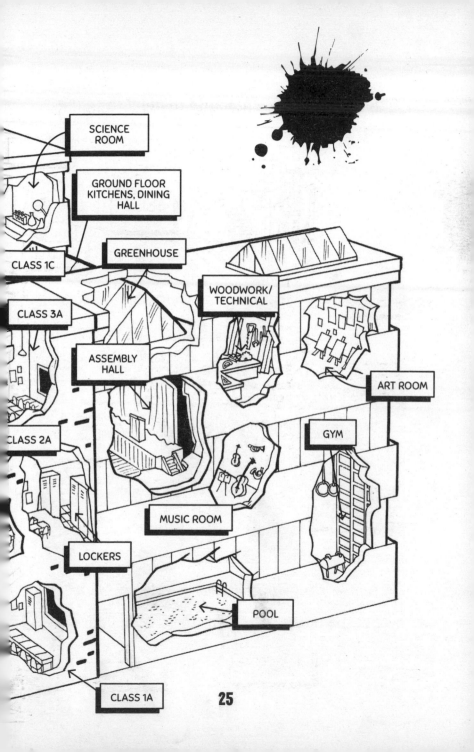

SCIENCE ROOM

GROUND FLOOR KITCHENS, DINING HALL

GREENHOUSE

WOODWORK/ TECHNICAL

CLASS 1C

CLASS 3A

ASSEMBLY HALL

ART ROOM

CLASS 2A

GYM

MUSIC ROOM

LOCKERS

POOL

CLASS 1A

25

JJ and Pie Face ran across to meet the gang. 'Hi everyone,' said JJ. 'Have you seen? The Super Epic Turbo Cricket Challenge Cup team has already been announced!'

JJ is the sportiest member of the gang. She can run faster, kick harder and jump higher than anyone else at Bash Street. She's also the school chess club's best player. She doesn't like chess, but she likes winning and loves beating Walter.

'What, already?! Let's check it out!' cried Pie Face.

Pie Face's real name is Peter, but he loves pies more than anything else, so he gets called Pie Face.

As the gang approached the school notice board, the noisy crowd around it fell silent and stepped aside. Two pieces of notebook paper had been pinned on the board.

One announced that all pupils were to go to the assembly hall at 9.00am to be bored rigid by Walter's dad. Well, that's not exactly what it said, but you get the meaning.

The second piece of paper was much more exciting!

Dennis stared. That '(C)' beside his name meant Miss Mistry had chosen him as the new Super Epic Turbo Cricket team captain.

Sweet.

'No one told me we had a game today,' said Dennis. 'I don't have my kit. I'm not even wearing my lucky underpants!'

'Or me,' said Rubi

'Why would you be wearing my lucky underpants?' said Dennis, grinning.

'Doofus,' said Rubi. 'I meant I don't have my kit either!'

The school bell rang. There was a loud **GROAN!** and the pupils started walking around the building to the entrance.

Dennis pulled Mandi to the side and pointed.

'Look, Mandi!' he said. 'It's the mayor!'

The mayor strode purposefully into the playground, swinging his briefcase. There was nothing inside it, but he thought it made him look important.

Dennis produced a pea-shooter from one of the pockets in his shorts and a little bottle from another.

'What's that?' whispered Pie Face.

'Cod liver oil capsules,' Dennis chuckled. 'Watch this!'

He expertly rolled a few of the capsules into his pea-shooter and raised it to his lips.

PUFF! The capsules flew silently across the playground and landed tamely in front of the school's front door.

'You missed,' Minnie scorned, though she was secretly relieved.

'No he didn't,' said Rubi. 'Watch!'

The mayor's next step crushed the capsules, squirting slippery fish oil in his own path. His feet slid away from under him. He cried out, threw his arms in the air and fell down the stairs.

'That was a very un-mayorly word!' said Mandi crossly. 'All the year ones will be saying it by the end of the day!'

#$@&%

They hurried over and helped the mayor to his feet, hoping to embarrass him even more.

'Are you alright, sir?' said Dennis, innocently. '**Thank cod** you didn't hurt yourself!'

'Hake care now,' said Rubi, as the mayor got to his feet gingerly. 'You've haddock a nasty fall.'

'Leave me alone!" snarled the mayor. He straightened his tie and his glasses and stomped into the school.

Minnie was holding her nose. 'He stinks of fish!' she laughed.

'**BLAMTASTIC!**' said Dennis, fist-bumping the gang. 'You know, I'd forgotten how much fun school can be!'

'Come on,' said Mandi. 'We'd better get to the assembly hall.'

Looks like today's gonna be great! – over-confident Ed

Chapter Three

THE MAYOR'S BIG NEWS!

'What's all this about, then?' asked Minnie, taking a seat beside Dennis in the assembly hall.

'Dunno,' said Dennis, 'but my timetable says we should be doing maths now, so I'm happy!'

On the stage in front of them stood Mr Belcher the headmaster, Mayor Brown, a small, grumpy-looking woman and a huge man with wide shoulders and strange glasses.

'Who are they?' asked Mandi.

'Never seen them before,' whispered Rubi.

The mayor stepped forward, only to be interrupted immediately.

The mayor glared at Bash Street School. Nervous pupils tried not to catch his eye.

'Just before the summer holidays,' the mayor started, 'this school failed its tenth inspection in a row. Mr Stamp, the school

inspector, happens to be allergic to
anything slimy, so to find his car
filled with frogspawn . . .'

Giggles broke out in the audience.
'. . . was a bit of a shock to his system,'
the mayor carried on. 'Thankfully, he has
made a full recovery, but . . .'

'What about the frogs?' someone called
out, and the audience dissolved into helpless
sniggering which turned into fake nose-blowing
and coughing.

'Enough! All the other mayors are laughing at
me,' said the mayor. 'They joke that I'm having a
night-mayor. Something must be done.'

'With immediate effect,' said the mayor
gravely, 'Mr Belcher will be . . . *retiring*.'

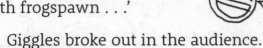

OOH! How dramatic!

34

Mr Belcher fell off his chair.

'But Mr Mayor!' cried Mr Belcher, crawling
toward the mayor. 'Don't make me retire!
My wife wants me to take dancing lessons,
and if I retire I won't have an excuse
not to!'

The many excuses of a reluctant ballroom dancer.

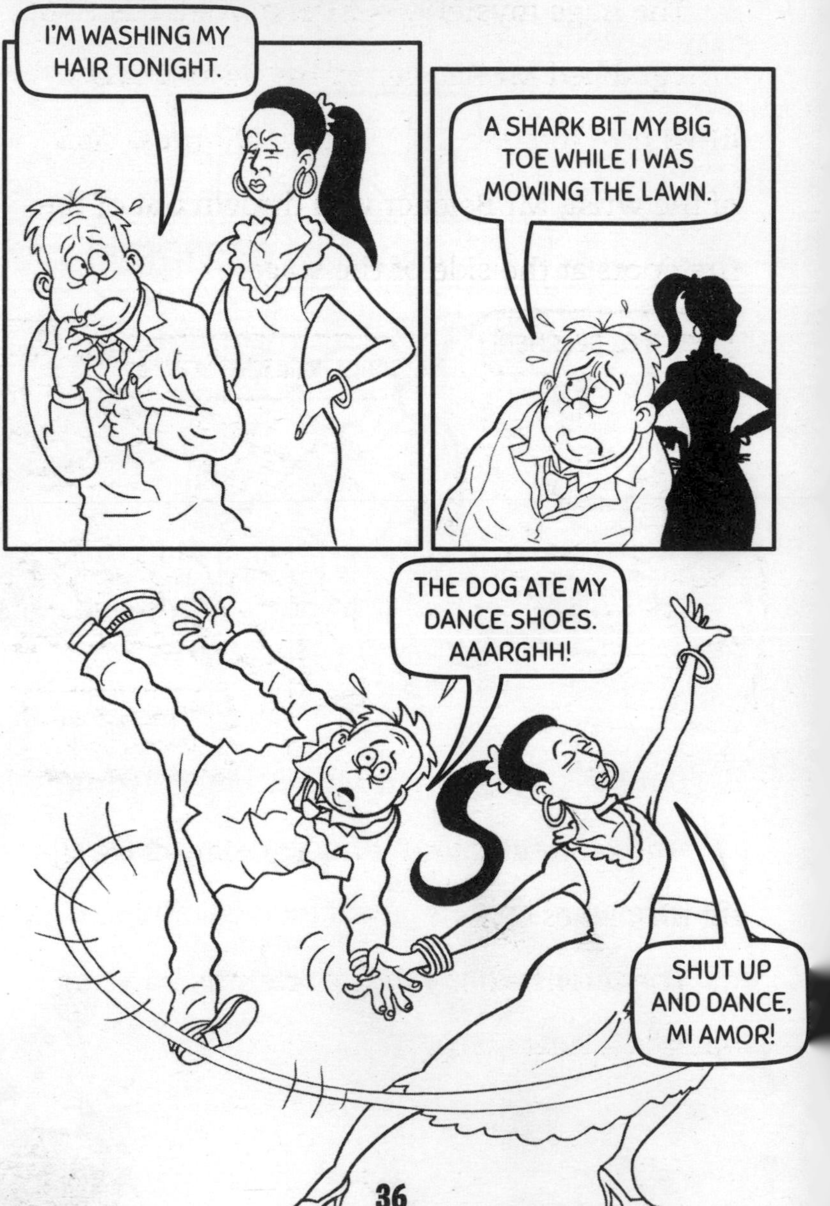
I'M WASHING MY HAIR TONIGHT.
A SHARK BIT MY BIG TOE WHILE I WAS MOWING THE LAWN.
THE DOG ATE MY DANCE SHOES. AAARGHH!
SHUT UP AND DANCE, MI AMOR!

The huge mysterious man moved. His right arm grabbed Mr Belcher by his tie and casually lifted him into the air. With an effortless flick of the wrist, Mr Belcher was thrown out of the fire doors at the side of the stage.

BYE–BYE, BELCHER!

NICE MEETING YOU!

CRASH!

These teachers are very polite.

'Happy retirement!' said the man, dusting off his gloves.

The pupils sat in silence, mouths hanging open in amazement.

'As I was saying,' said the mayor, 'Mr Belcher is . . . has retired. Mrs Clamp here . . .' he gestured to the grumpy-looking woman, 'will be your new, improved head teacher.'

The mayor then pointed to the man who had just thrown the old head teacher out of the school. 'And Mr Fayle will become Bash Street's first ever ***Master of Behavioural Remedies.***'

'What does Behavioural Remedies even mean?' mumbled Pie Face.

'Not a clue, but I've got a bad feeling we're about to find out,' said Dennis.

The mayor sat down and Mrs Clamp stood up.

'Students, there are going to be big changes around here,' she said. 'You'll find out about them later. But first, there's the annual Super Epic Turbo Cricket match. Beanotown Academy will undoubtedly win again, of course, but being reminded that you're losers never hurt anyone.'

'It hurts me,' growled JJ.

As they filed out of the hall, Mandi looked worried.

'Cheer up,' said Minnie. 'We've seen off plenty of teachers before, how hard can a head teacher be?'

'I don't know,' said Mandi, 'but the mayor's never made changes like this before. There's something fishy going on here, and I'm not talking about the cod liver oil on his shoes.'

They rushed round to the PE block where Miss Mistry, Bash Street's Super Epic Turbo Cricket team coach and the school's most popular teacher, was waiting for them.

MISS MISTRY

'Hurry up, you lot,' she said. 'Kick-off is in five minutes.'

'We didn't know there was a game on, Miss,' said Mandi.

'Neither did I until I got here,' said Miss Mistry. 'Go and get changed.'

'Dennis doesn't have his underpants,' said Minnie, 'and I didn't bring my taser.'

'Tasers are banned,' said Miss Mistry, giving her a stern look, 'after the unfortunate incident with the line judge last season.'

> She's fine now. Well, just about. – Reassuring Ed.

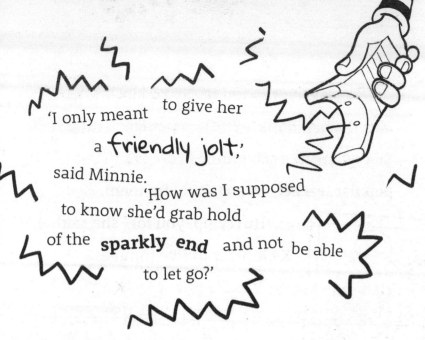

'I only meant to give her a **friendly jolt**,' said Minnie. 'How was I supposed to know she'd grab hold of the **sparkly end** and not be able to let go?'

The Beanotown Academy players were big, strong and unfairly healthy.

None of them are missing their lucky underpants, thought Dennis. *They definitely knew about the game before this morning.* **That's not fair!**

'Do you know Mrs Clamp and Mr Fayle?' Mandi asked Miss Mistry.

'Not really,' replied Miss Mistry. 'Mrs Clamp was the deputy head at Beanotown Academy. She's wanted to be the head for years, but it looks like Mr Glass-Ceiling will never retire. She's known as the strictest teacher of all time.'

'Mr Fayle is her right-hand man. They've worked together forever. He's known as the cruellest teacher of all time, but

THE COAT!
Cruellest Of
All Time!

RULES

THE STOAT!
Strictest Teacher
Of All time!

Mmm...not the
scariest nicknames
ever, but I guess
Academy pupils don't
get out much!

he's volunteered to referee the game,

so I suppose he can't be all bad.'

Miss Mistry walked off to shake hands with Mr Fayle.

Dennis couldn't take his eyes off the huge teacher.

He couldn't put his finger on it

but something wasn't quite right.

Dennis shivered.

'What's up?' asked Mandi.

'I felt a great disturbance in the force,' said Dennis.

'You are such a weirdo,' interrupted Minnie.

'Come on. Let's crush these losers.'

Mandi turned and noticed Fayle staring at Dennis. She could see Fayle's face reddening.

Thin wisps of smoke were escaping from his ears.

He doesn't seem like a very nice person, she thought, then trotted onto the pitch.

Chapter Four

SUPER EPIC TURBO CRICKET

THE HISTORY OF SUPER EPIC TURBO CRICKET

Super Epic Turbo Cricket was invented in 1938 by a Bash Street pupil called Pansy Potter. Girls weren't allowed to play football in 1938, so Pansy decided to invent a new sport that everyone could play.

The recipe for Super Epic Turbo Cricket was simple. Take all the best bits of football, add a dash of ice hockey, a sprinkling of rugby, a healthy slug of cage-fighting, then garnish with fresh paintball. Basically, Pansy cooked up the ultimate mutant supersport.

She called it . . . Super Epic Turbo Riot.

Then she changed her mind and called it Super Epic Turbo Cricket because she knew teachers would never let kids play a sport with 'Riot' in its name. And she decided goals scored from a player's own half

should be worth two points,

because . . . well,

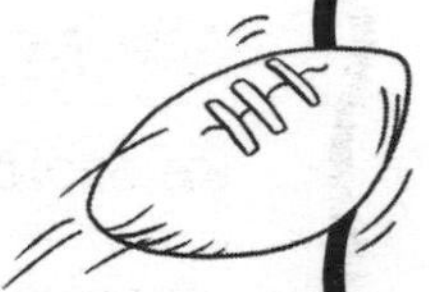

★★★ **EPIC!** ★★★

On the other hand, teachers do like cricket. No one gets bruised playing cricket, unless they nod off and land on their face. Super Epic Turbo Cricket awards bonus points for bruises. Yes, it's that kind of game.

OUCH!

The whole school lined the pitch, hoping for a chance to throw an egg at one of the Academy players.

Beanotown Academy had won the Challenge Cup for the last fourteen years, so no one gave Bash Street much of a chance. Even Minnie was really only hoping to win if the game finished in a draw and had to be settled by a bruise count. She figured she could always give herself a few to boost their chances.

BARBARA BUTTSQUEAK

TIM DIMM

PEREGRINE POT-ROAST

JOYCE FOYCE

SPOTTY SPUDKIN

BARRY BULLWHIP

48

The game was hard-fought from the start. The Academy took the lead early when Minnie hit Scotty Spudskin's hand with her face, injuring him and giving away a penalty.

The crowd groaned when Tim Dimm thumped the ball past Rubi and into the net.

Then Bash Street went two down when Barbara Buttsqueak sat on Stevie Starr, letting the unmarked Tim Dimm flash the ball past Rubi into the net. It was a definite foul. The crowd booed, but Mr Fayle let the goal stand. He was doing his old school team a favour or two!

In the second half, Dennis pulled a point back when he shoulder-charged Peregrine Pot-Roast, hid the ball up his jumper and ran it into the goal before anyone noticed. The crowd went wild, sensing a comeback on the

cards, but with thirty seconds on the clock
Bash Street would need to act quick to snatch
the win.

'I'm beat, cuz,' panted Minnie to Dennis.
'I'm going to pretend I'm injured so Miss
Mistry can bring Mandi on.'

'OK,' Dennis nodded. 'Fresh legs would
be good. What kind of injury did you have
in m–'

'**MY EYES!**' screamed Minnie.
'I'M BLIND!'

Miss Mistry rushed onto the pitch with her
first aid bag.

'What happened, Minnie?'

'Who said that?' cried Minnie, flailing
around and almost slapping Joyce Foyce on
the side of the head.

Minnie never does anything by halves,
thought Dennis, as Miss Mistry led her off the
pitch and signalled Mandi to take her place.

'Not much time to go,' Dennis said to
Mandi. 'I'll pass the ball to you from the restart.

Get ready to launch a Mandi Meteor, okay?'

Mandi nodded . . . cautiously. She'd secretly hoped to be an unused substitute.

Mr Fayle blew his whistle to restart the game. Dennis dropped the ball behind him, back-heeled it to Mandi, then set off towards Academy's goal at top speed.

Mandi fumbled the ball and almost dropped it.

Oh, crumbs she thought. *What if I get tackled?*

Academy players charged towards her, grinning as if to say, 'we're going to enjoy this'.

What if I throw it straight to one of them instead of to Dennis, Mandi thought, clutching the ball to her tummy.

Academy players closed in on her from every direction.

She shut her eyes. *What's the worst that can happen, Mandi?* she thought. *You can do it!*

Mandi launched the ball as hard as she could in Dennis's direction. Four Academy players leapt to tackle her as the ball left her hand.

Mandi ducked, and rolled.

The ball flew high over Dennis's head, but he chased it anyway. Barry Bullwhip, the Academy goalkeeper, charged off his line, eyes fixed on the ball.

This is going to hurt, said one bit of Dennis's brain.

Don't listen to him, Dennis. All your friends will be happy if you score, said another bit of his brain. *You can do it!*

The second bit of his brain won. Dennis
kept running so fast that his heels were
kicking him on the butt.

'Dennis will never catch that,' groaned
Minnie. Miss Mistry looked at her sharply.

'I've a sixth sense for what's happening
on the pitch,' said Minnie. 'Well, a fifth sense,
I suppose. Now that I'm blind.'

Then Dennis's left leg decided it would
rather be on the right. Dennis tripped over
it, hit the ground and rolled . . . right into the
path of Barry Bullwhip, who still had his nose
in the air, and was still charging forward.

CRUMP!

Barry fell over Dennis, landing face-first
on the muddy penalty spot. Dennis stopped
rolling just in time to see Mandi's Meteor

bounce once . . .   then twice . . .

before coming to rest just over the line.

Two points. Bash Street were in the lead!

Mr Fayle checked his watch.

'Oh dear, I'm terribly sorry,' he said, 'but time was up before . . .'

'Ahem!'

Miss Mistry glared at him, tapping her own watch to show she knew exactly how much time was left.

Mr Fayle blew his whistle, angrily.

'Bash Street win,' he said, unhappily.

'It's a miracle!' cried Minnie, leaping off the bench. Miss Mistry folded her arms.

'Er . . . a miracle that I can see again!' added Minnie, dashing off to celebrate.

The crowd carried Mandi off the field
in triumph.

'Well played,' Miss Mistry said to
Mr Fayle. 'Better luck next time.'

Dennis noticed she had her fingers crossed
behind her back. *Miss Mistry is all right*, he
thought.

Fayle grunted, but never looked at Miss Mistry. Instead, he glared at Dennis, his eyes glowing red with fury.

Miss Mistry clapped her hands to get everyone's attention.

'Everyone get changed and head back to class, please,' she said.

As he walked to the changing rooms, Dennis could still feel Fayle's angry stare burning into the back of his head. He didn't care. He was a winner.

Chapter Five

THE TEACHER WHO'S TOO COOL FOR SCHOOL

'What's going on, Miss?' asked Dennis when they were all back in Class 3C. 'Has Mr Belcher really been sacked because I . . . er, someone . . . put frogspawn in the inspector's car?'

'How will Mrs Clamp do better than Mr Belcher did? Is everything going to change?' said Mandi, quietly.

Miss Mistry sighed. 'Try not to worry, Mandi. Change is not always a bad thing. You're some of the smartest, most creative pupils I've ever taught. I just think the mayor doesn't like the way we do things here.'

'He prefers the way the Academy works. Strict rules. Uniforms. No questions. At the Academy, the students really think the teachers are the most important people in the school.'

'The thing is that you're all Bash Street kids,' she continued. 'You aren't like Academy pupils. Shouting at you to sit down, be quiet and get on with it doesn't get the best out of you. I should know – I was a pupil here. I'm a Bash Street kid too.'

'The school's job . . . my job . . . is to help you all to become the best you can be. You'll all succeed in your own ways. I really believe that.'

'You can tell all that to Mrs Clamp, can't you?' said Rubi. 'It sounds really inspiring to me.'

Miss Mistry shook her head.

'I think she'd just tell me to sit down, be quiet and get on with it,' said Miss Mistry. 'And that's why . . . maybe . . . I'll have to leave Bash Street School soon. I have a choice that you don't. I'm only forced to go to a school when I work in one, but I don't want to be part of a school that tries to turn you all into little robots.'

WHAT'S WRONG WITH ROBOTS?!

'That is absolute guffbombs,' exploded Dennis. 'You'd never do that! You're the only teacher I ever didn't really, really dislike! Promise you won't go . . . at least until we know what we're up against! We need you here. This is just a **treacherous takeover by terrible teachers!**'

'Good use of alliteration, Dennis,' sniffed Miss Mistry. 'I've taught you well.'

'Alli-what?' Dennis whispered to Rubi, behind his hand.

Something to do with alligators, right?

Miss Mistry wiped her nose, then her
eyes, then her nose again. Mandi shuddered.
People are so unhygienic when
they're upset.

'Okay,' nodded Miss Mistry.

UGH!!

'I'll give it a few weeks. But we're
all going to have to be very careful not to draw
any attention to ourselves.'

The door of Class 3C crashed open and
Mr Fayle strode in. He was carrying a laptop,
which he plugged into the whiteboard. A slide
appeared on the screen. Fayle turned to face
the class.

'Mrs Clamp has asked me to issue some
new school rules, which **Will Be Obeyed**,'
he said. 'She calls them her Five Absolute Rules
for Taming Schools.'

Dennis's eyes opened wide.

F.A.R.T.S? Really? Was this a joke?

Fayle clicked to the next slide. Dennis

wasn't surprised to find Clamp's **F.A.R.T.S.**

stank the school out.

NO FUN (EXCEPT ON FUNDAYS)

NO SPEAKING UNLESS SPOKEN TO

NO THINKING UNAUTHORISED
THOUGHTS

NO EXCUSES

NO PETS

'FYI, sir,' said JJ. 'Funday isn't a real day.'

'I know,' said Fayle. 'That's the whole point.
School is not about fun. It's about results!'

'Make sure you look at these too,' he said
as he left the classroom, leaving a piece of
paper on Walter's desk. He picked it up, read it
joyfully and passed it on to Minnie.

'These probably apply to people like you
more than me, it's a list of consequences for
anyone who doesn't follow Fayle's **F.A.R.T.S.**,'
he said.

MR FAYLE'S PERFECT PUNISHMENTS

1. CLEAN OUT JANITOR'S TOENAIL CLIPPINGS DRAWER
2. CLEAN THE TEACHERS' TOILET
3. SERVE TEA AND BISCUITS IN THE STAFF ROOM
4. GIVE MRS CLAMP A MANICURE
5. CUT THE GRASS – WITH SCISSORS
6. WEAR THE 'STUPID' EMOJI ON YOUR FOREHEAD ALL DAY
7. GIVE WINSTON, THE SCHOOL CAT, A BATH
8. OIL MR FAYLE'S ARMPITS
9. DANCE THE SCHOOL DANCE WITH MRS CLAMP

Dennis hated rules. He hated being told what to do. He hated being told what not to do. But more than anything, Dennis hated being punished for breaking someone else's stupid rules. And he thought these rules were really, really stupid.

The bell rang for lunch.

'Miss Mistry's right,' Dennis
said to his friends as they made
their way to the dining hall.
'We've got to fight
this with everything we've got.'

'That's literally
the exact opposite
of what she said,' Rubi pointed out.

'I was reading between the lines,'
said Dennis.

Chapter Six

SINGING FROM THE SAME GRIM SHEET

Lunch was a gloomy affair. Mr Belcher wasn't exactly the gang's favourite adult, but everyone felt sorry for him. If he didn't want to learn how to do the Argentinian tango, why should he?

'Do you get other kinds of tango?' asked Pie Face, spooning rhubarb soup into his mouth. 'Maybe he'd prefer the Irish tango?'

'Forget Belcher,' said Minnie.

THEIR FARTS HAVE TAKEN THE LAST BIT OF FUN OUT OF SCHOOL! WHAT ARE WE GOING TO DO ABOUT CLAMP AND FAYLE?

'We're going to show them you can't stop a Bash Street kid having fun!' said Dennis, biting into a crispy kipper pancake.

'How?' asked Mandi.

'We'll just carry on like we always do,' he grinned. 'Who cares about rules and punishments? It's pranks, jokes and laughs all the way!'

When they got back to class, Miss Mistry had filled the whiteboard with some very odd stuff indeed.

'What's that, Miss?' asked Dennis, puzzled.

'It's the new school song,' she said. 'We've all got to learn it by heart and sing it

first thing every morning. It's supposed to motivate us. There's a whole-school practice in –' She checked her watch. 'Two minutes.'

Dennis's heart sank. So did his stomach, lungs, liver, kidneys and whatever other organs he had too. *A school song? Just like the Academy*, he thought.

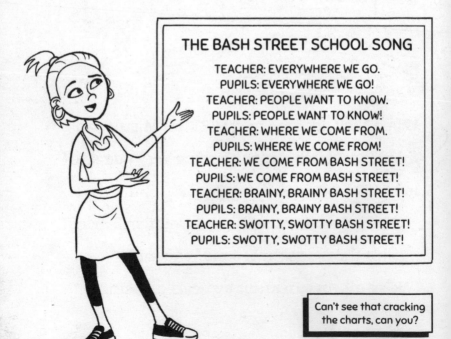

THE BASH STREET SCHOOL SONG

TEACHER: EVERYWHERE WE GO.
PUPILS: EVERYWHERE WE GO!
TEACHER: PEOPLE WANT TO KNOW.
PUPILS: PEOPLE WANT TO KNOW!
TEACHER: WHERE WE COME FROM.
PUPILS: WHERE WE COME FROM!
TEACHER: WE COME FROM BASH STREET!
PUPILS: WE COME FROM BASH STREET!
TEACHER: BRAINY, BRAINY BASH STREET!
PUPILS: BRAINY, BRAINY BASH STREET!
TEACHER: SWOTTY, SWOTTY BASH STREET!
PUPILS: SWOTTY, SWOTTY BASH STREET!

Can't see that cracking the charts, can you?

The school bell gave out four short rings, meaning everyone had to go to the assembly hall immediately.

DRING!

THE BASH STREET SCHOOL BELL

1 ring = Beginning/end of class
2 rings = Janitor to the school office, please
3 rings = Head teacher announcement
4 rings = All staff and pupils to the assembly hall
5 rings = The staff toilets are blocked again
6 rings = Sprout curry is on the dinner menu
7 rings = One of our guinea pigs is missing
8 rings = School bell testing
9 rings = Vomit in the corridor alert
10+ rings = Winston the school cat is playing with the button again

Mrs Clamp and Mr Fayle were standing on the stage when they arrived, waiting for silence. Mr Fayle stepped forward and commanded the school like an army drill sergeant, 'Repeat after me!'

He chanted the first line of the song,

'Everywhere we go.' Reluctantly, the pupils repeated it. After a slow start, Mr Fayle chanted louder and faster with every line.

Every time the pupils thought they'd finished, Fayle started over again. Soon the pupils were caught up in the song. When the

AND AGAIN! MAKE SOME NOISE!

bell rang for the end of the day, they were still singing. Fayle was relentless. They'd done 208 verses. Every so often he'd yell, 'Louder!' after his line.

Dennis had a sore throat. Mandi had a sore head. Minnie had sore eyebrows from all the glaring she'd done. Nobody was enjoying any of it.

Well, hardly anybody . . .

HE'S A DANCING FOOL!

I JUST CAN'T... I JUST CAN'T... I JUST CAN'T CONTROL MY FEET!

Crumbs! Walter's gone full Riverdance!

Gnasher put his paws over his ears and howled, but not even his loudest werewolf impersonation could drown out the awful din.

Finally, ten minutes after the last bell had rung, the song was over. The kids slumped back into their seats.

At least tomorrow couldn't be as bad as today.

Could it? Dennis wasn't going to take any chances!

'Secret meeting in the haunted basement,' he said to Minnie. 'In five minutes. Pass it on.'

Just behind them, Walter smirked. He knew someone who would like to know about this meeting.

Chapter Seven

THE MISTRY MOB

The basement wasn't haunted. Dennis made that up so he could use it as a secret hideout. It was dark, though, and there was a creaky old trapdoor in the floor. Mandi always had her torch on full beam, just in case.

CLAMP AND FAYLE WANT TO KNOCK ALL THE FUN OUT OF SCHOOL, BUT IF WE STICK TOGETHER, WE CAN DEFEAT THEM!

'I agree,' nodded Minnie.

'But what can we do?' asked Mandi.

'Show them they can't stop Bash Street kids having fun,' said Dennis. '**Muck about more than ever before!** We could form a prank army so the fun never stops.'

'That'll ruffle their feathers,' said Pie Face.

'We need a cool name and a motto,' said Rubi.

'Minnie's Minions', said Minnie

'What about Bash Street Baddies?' suggested JJ.

'**The Mistry Mob!**' said Mandi.

'That's good,' Dennis said, followed by nods of approval.

WELL SAID!

Mandi clapped excitedly, then stopped in case it was uncool.

'Stick together is a good motto,' said JJ.

'But what exactly are we fighting for?' asked Rubi.

THE MISTRY MOB
STICK TOGETHER!

Dennis thought. 'We want our school back.'

'And how exactly do we get it?' asked JJ.

Dennis paused. He wasn't really a details sort of guy.

'The mayor wanted Bash Street to be more like the Academy,' Mandi said. 'That's why he put Academy teachers in charge. What if Bash Street got worse, and not better?'

'He'd hate that!' said Dennis.

'He might do a U-turn!' said Mandi.

Dennis waved everyone in for a Mistry Mob huddle.

'The fight starts here!' Dennis said. 'We're gonna laugh Clamp and Fayle right out of this school.'

They put their hands together and did the secret Mistry Mob handshake . . .

'Remember,' said Dennis. 'As long as we stick together, we can't . . . '

'Fayle!' interrupted Minnie.

'**Exactly!**' said Dennis.

'No,' said Minnie, pointing over his shoulder. 'Mr Fayle . . . behind you!'

Massive Fayle, with his eerie red eyes and super-strength, was standing in the doorway. How had he known they were there?

Fayle advanced, rubbing his hands together.

'WALTER SQUEALED ON US!' growled Dennis.

'A secret meeting, eh?' he said. 'Well, I don't like secrets.'

Fayle stepped onto the trapdoor, which

creaked loudly. Another step. The wood

cracked. Fayle looked down anxiously, then

fell through

the

shattered

trapdoor!

'Leg it!' cried Minnie. And they did.

Dennis waited to make sure no kid was left

behind. As he turned to leave, Fayle emerged

from the hole, propelled upwards by flaming

jets in the soles of his shoes. His goggles

glowed. It was pretty awesome, Dennis had

to admit.

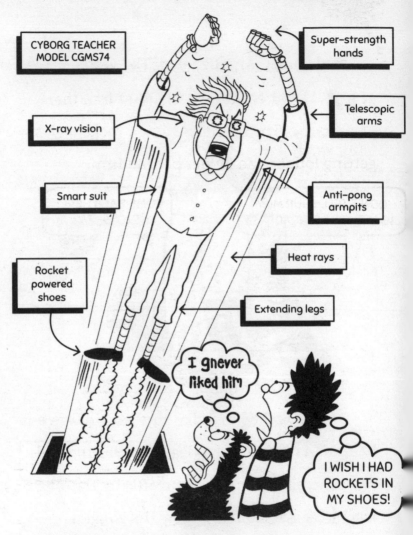

'OMG!' he breathed. 'Fayle is half-teacher, half-robot! He's a tea-bot!'

Dennis ran upstairs, Gnasher racing ahead of him. He burst through the door into the playground. The sound of Fayle's rockets was getting louder and louder behind him.

DON'T TELL YOUR MUM WHAT HE SAID, READERS!

COME BACK HERE, YOU #$@&%!

Even I'll have to look that one up in the dictionary!

'He's after us!' cried Dennis.

There was a coughing sound, a *PHUT!*, then silence. The ominous thumping of an angry teacher's footsteps took over. Dennis risked a look over his shoulder.

'He's out of fuel!' he laughed.

Fayle grabbed a bike from the rack, jumped on and pedalled after them. He was really quick!

As Fayle edged closer, Dennis could feel his eyes burning into him.

'We'll never make it to the gate, Gnasher,' cried Dennis. 'We have to go over the wall!'

They veered left, aiming at the tall school wall. Fayle laughed. He had them cornered now!

Gnasher cleared the wall in a single bound. Dennis leaped as high as he could, hooked one elbow over, then the other. Gnasher grabbed his jumper with his teeth and heaved. They toppled over the top. They'd made it!

Wow, thought Dennis as they ran home. *A cyborg teacher with superpowers. It's like an awesome movie I'm not old enough to watch!*

Later, Dennis sat with his thumbs in a bowl of ice-cold water. They were red hot after some high speed texting action.

The Mistry Mob group chat

Dennis: guess wot i fnd out? Fayle has jets in his hands and feet! Cyborg teacher!

Minnie: u sure, cuz? U know u sometimes get carried away . . .

Mandi: omg! I drew a character like that in a comic once. Do u think this is my fault? Like i created him? 😮

Dennis: no!

Minnie: no!

Mandi: phew!

Rubi: did u c a brand on the jets? I wouldn't mind some of them.

Dennis: r u serious?

Rubi: no!

Rubi: as if!

Rubi: but did u c a brand?

Dennis: no, and 4 some reason i didn't want 2 ask! Try imafreakycyborg.com!

Rubi: my dad tried 2 make a cyborg in his lab. He built the robot part, but no1 volunteered 2 be the human bit. Can't think why . . .

Dennis: we need 2 launch our rebellion 2moro. If we let c and f get comfy, it will be much harder 2 get rid of them.

Minnie: nvr underestimate a teacher with jets in their hands and feet, that's what i always say.

Dennis: u've literally nvr said that before in ur life.

Minnie: i think it all the time, tho! U can't prove i don't!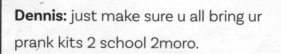

Dennis: just make sure u all bring ur prank kits 2 school 2moro.

Minnie: ok

Mandi: ok 👍

Rubi: ok

Pie face: ok

Minnie: pie face, how long have u been on chat? U haven't said 1 word!

Pie face: i can't type as quickly as you lot. I always wanted to meet a real cyborg. Just not at school.

Dennis dried his fingers on his pyjamas, and typed one last message.

Dennis: the battle 4 bash street has **begun**!

Chapter Eight

PRANKSDAY!

The next morning, the Mistry Mob went to school early to set up their pranks.

SHOCKER!

They sneaked in through the Janitor's door, which was easy because he was asleep in his office.

Weighed down by school bags full of prank kits, the Mob split up. Dennis and Rubi took the second floor, Minnie and Mandi took the first and Pie Face and JJ took the ground floor. They each got to work setting up the teacher prank-traps they'd prepared the night before.

Ten minutes later, they met up again in the entrance hall. Except Pie Face and JJ.

'Where are they?' fretted Mandi. 'The teachers will arrive soon.'

Dennis was worried. 'If they see us, they'll know we set the traps.'

'Let's leave them,' said Minnie, heading for the door.

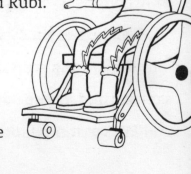

'Hey!' said Mandi. 'We stick together, remember?'

'I hear footsteps,' said Rubi.

'I knew they'd come,' said Minnie.

JJ appeared first, trainers squealing on the

shiny floor. Pie Face was hot on her tail.

'Fayle's coming!' hissed JJ.

They ran out into the playground, and hid behind the recycling bins.

'Did he see you?' panted Dennis.

'Don't think so,' said JJ. 'We heard him coming and legged it.'

'We got it done, though,' said Pie Face.

'Great,' said Dennis. 'Now we wait for the fun to begin.'

❋ ❋ ❋

'Pranksday' was the funniest day in Bash Street School's history.

The fun started at break time. A bucket of whipped cream had been balanced on top of the tuck shop door. When Mr Fayle opened it, the bucket toppled onto his head.

UGH! DRIPPY!

SPLAT!

Fayle was furious. He ordered an immediate locker inspection to identify the prankster.

When he found a smear of whipped cream on locker 13, he thought he'd struck gold. But

when he undid the latch, the door flew open and a custard pie shot out and splatted him in the face.

UGH! LUMPY!

SPLOOEY!

Fayle spluttered and squelched his way to the school office, wiping custard from his eyes.

JUST UGH!

Mrs Yodel offered to wipe him down with a damp sponge, only to discover her cleaning sponge had been switched for a sponge cake.

I'M SORRY, MR FA–HA–HA–FAYLE! LOOKS LIKE I'VE BEEN PRANKED TOO.

SMEAR!

Meanwhile, Mrs Clamp was shivering in her office. She briefly wondered what all the noise from the office was about, then decided she didn't care.

She pressed the button to turn her heating up. There was a *CLONK*, a *WHIRR*, then a loud, wet . . .

SPLUDGE!

Mrs Clamp was covered in wet, green slime.

SHRIEEEEK!!!

Mrs Clamp dashed out of her office.

'What happened?' Mr Fayle cried.

'I'm not sure,' Mrs Clamp said. 'I just turned on the heating and got covered in this stuff!'

Mrs Clamp looked at Mr Fayle. 'Never mind me – what happened to you?'

'I was attacked with whipped cream, splatted with custard and then sponged,' he said.

He wiped some slime from Mrs Clamp's expensive suit and tasted it.

'Lime jelly,' he said.

JELLY, SPONGES, CUSTARD AND CREAM? MR FAYLE, WE'RE BEING **TRIFLED** WITH!

95

Clamp and Fayle stepped back into her office. The door slammed shut.

Dennis and the gang, hiding behind the enormous cheese plant that Mrs Yodel kept in the entrance hall, dissolved into helpless laughter.

'Did you get all of that, Rubi?' asked
Dennis.

A tiny buzzing drone landed in Rubi's lap.
'Every second is now uploaded to my private
online channel!' she giggled.

They high-fived and whooped, until
Mrs Yodel stuck her head out of her office
and told them to run along.

The rest of the day was
filled with epic pranks.
Clamp and Fayle
were slimed, oozed,
egged, cling-filmed, feathered,
floured, air-horned, oiled, wormed
and de-wormed.

Mr Fayle eventually tried to hide in the staff toilet, only to find out someone had switched the **MALE** and **FEMALE** signs.

Olive the dinner lady chased him out of there with a week-old French loaf.

As the gang walked home, they watched the videos on Rubi's tablet.

'That was great,' said Rubi. 'But how does it help us stop the mayor's plans?'

'Today is just the beginning. We'll get our chance,' said Dennis. 'The important thing is to be ready when it comes.'

'Hello, losers,' a sneering voice said. They all groaned.

'I know who pulled those pranks today,' said Walter. 'It was you, wasn't it?'

'Isn't there someone else you could annoy?' said Rubi. 'Oh, I forgot you don't have any friends because you're so mean to everyone!'

'I'll have lots of new friends soon,' said Walter. 'When we join the Academy!'

He laughed at their shocked faces.

'That's right. My father has wanted to close Bash Street School for years. Mr Testy, the new school inspector, is visiting on Friday to see how Mrs Clamp and Mr Fayle are getting on.'

'When he sees how much better the school

is, he'll say the Academy should take over completely. Bash Street School will be gone forever, and we'll all be Academy pupils. Daddy will make a tidy profit by turning the building into a celebrity soft play centre. He says the money he makes will pay for a spray tan booth in his office. Which is nice.'

They walked away, leaving Walter alone.

'Enjoy the rest of the week,' he called after them, mockingly. 'Friday will be the last day you can call yourselves Bash Street kids!'

'Did you hear that?' said Mandi. 'There's no hope now!'

'WRONG!' said Dennis, grinning. 'Walter doesn't realise it, but he just told us what we needed to know.'

FRIDAY IS OUR CHANCE TO SAVE BASH STREET SCHOOL!

Chapter Nine

FAYLE'S REVENGE

Fayle didn't know who'd pranked him but he knew what he was going to do about it. Anyone who ignored **F.A.R.T.S.** would suffer instant punishment of the most horrible kind.

Pie Face was Fayle's first victim. When he asked Olive the dinner lady if she could save him some of her world-famous Pie-in-a-pie Pie, he broke the first of Fayle's F.A.R.T.S.

Pie Face's punishment for talking was to bake himself a puff pastry PE kit. When he ran onto the Super Epic Turbo Cricket pitch later

that day, poor Pie Face was pounced on by a
pack of pesky pastry-pecking pigeons.

And, because Olive asked Fayle to go easy
on Pie Face, she was also punished. She had to
write I WILL NOT SPEAK WITHOUT BEING SPOKEN TO
one hundred times, using alphabet spaghetti
letters.

Rubi was then caught thinking about the
solar system when she should have been doing
long division. Her punishment
was to invent something
that would make people's
lives worse,
not better.

BOING!

Nobody
liked Rubi's
Bouncy-Staircase much.

When a painting of Clamp and Fayle was found on the wall of the girls' toilet, Minnie was made to paint over it . . . using her eyebrows.

'How did they know it was me?' she complained.

'Maybe if you hadn't signed your name at the bottom, you'd have got away with it?' suggested JJ.

Dennis had never been great at not breaking rules . . .

UNDERSTATEMENT ALERT!!

. . . so he soon found himself on the wrong end of one of Clamp's **F.A.R.T.S.** too . . .

He was playing games on his phone when he shouldn't have been, and he didn't notice Mr Fayle coming into Class 3C.

He also didn't notice Walter putting his hand up either, or him telling Mr Fayle that 'that horrid Dennis' was playing games in class.

'WHAT ARE YOU DOING, BOY ?'

boomed Mr Fayle into Dennis's left ear. Dennis DID notice that.

'I have fat fingeritis,' said Dennis. 'The doctor says I have to play games once an hour or I'll get sausage fingers!'

Gnasher jumped onto the desk. **Sausages? Yes please!** he thought.

Mr Fayle's mind was officially **BLOWN**! He'd waited twenty years for someone to break the *NO PETS* rule.

'Is that your dog?' he whispered. The lenses in his goggles whirred, zooming in and out on Gnasher.

'I've never seen that dog before in my life,' said Dennis. 'Right, Gnasher?'

Gnasher licked him on the cheek.

And then licked Mr Fayle. On the <u>**mouth**</u>.

'You insolent rascal! You'll pay for this . . . just as soon as I figure out how. I'll be right back!' screamed Mr Fayle, as he fled, clawing doggy drool

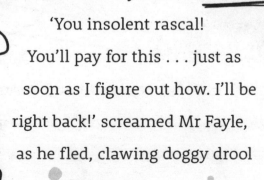

out of his mouth with his fingers.

'I think you've done it this time, Dennis,' said Miss Mistry, patting Gnasher on the head.

Dennis groaned.

Shortly, a damp-looking Mr Fayle returned. He walked purposefully to Dennis's desk, and extended his arm, like a footy referee pointing to the penalty spot, stopping a millimetre from Dennis's nose. There was a tiny sticky note in his hand.

Dennis had to cross his eyes to read what was written on it.

YOU'RE
NOT
FIRED

'Huh?' said Dennis. 'I'm not fired?'

'That's right,' said Fayle. 'But because of you, Dennis . . .'

He turned and pointed at Miss Mistry.

'. . . she IS!'

'Your class is a disgrace,' he said to her. 'They were behind the outrageous pranking yesterday, and it's all because **you** can't keep control of them! Get your things, Miss Mistry – you're histry! Er, history!'

The History of Bash Street School

REVISED EDITION

NEW CHAPTER: THE MISTRY MYSTERY

WORST OF ALL, I LET MYSELF DOWN.

EDITED BY DAI WILL FAYLE

That's one book I won't be pre-ordering!

The bell rang. It was home time.

No one moved. No one made a sound.

Miss Mistry stared grimly at Mr Fayle.
His face was redder than Dennis's maths
homework after marking.

'Class dismissed,' she said quietly.

The room was empty in less than a second.

'This is awful,' said Mandi as they walked
home. 'We got Miss Mistry the sack!'

'No,' said Minnie. 'Dennis got her the sack.'

'Gee! Thanks a lot, Min,' said Dennis,
rolling his eyes.

'What will we do now?' asked Rubi.

'We've still got a chance,' said Dennis. 'We
can fix this.'

'Look,' said JJ, pointing back towards the school gates.

Miss Mistry was standing by the kerb, holding a cardboard box. A woman pulled up in a little yellow car and Miss Mistry got in. The driver gave her a hug, and then they were gone.

'Poor Miss Mistry,' said Mandi.

The inspection is tomorrow,' said Dennis. 'Clamp and Fayle fail if the school fails. If we fail to fail, Fayle wins.'

'Simples!' said Minnie.

Dennis turned to Rubi. 'I need to speak to you about a special prank, Rubi. The time has come for . . .'

Chapter Ten

PRANKMAGEDDON!

It's not a made up word!

It was five to nine in the morning. Mrs Clamp and Mr Fayle were waiting for Mr Testy, the school inspector, in the lobby.

'You're sure there won't be more pranks today?' Mrs Clamp asked.

'Relax!' said Fayle. 'I'll make sure those troublemakers from Class 3C are out of the way and our new, improved pupils will take their places. And Miss Mistry's gone too.'

'She was far too soft,' nodded Mrs Clamp.

'She actually thought school should be fun!'

A man in a suit walked in. He was carrying a clipboard.

'That must be him,' said Fayle, walking away. 'You show him around. I'll arrange everything and join you later.'

He ran off down the corridor.

'Mr Testy!' cried Mrs Clamp, turning to the inspector, 'Welcome to Bash Street School!'

Fayle sprinted upstairs. He thought about using his shoe rockets, but they were too noisy. He stuck his head into Class 3C.

'Dennis, Minnie, Jem, Rubi, Mandi and Peter,' he said. 'Come to the basement.'

Jem was JJ's real name, and Peter was Pie

Face's. If a grown-up uses your real name,
it means you're **IN TROUBLE**.

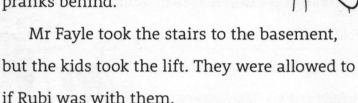

'Uh-oh!' whispered Mandi.
'What's this about?'

'Take your bags with you,'
said Minnie. 'We can't leave our
pranks behind.'

Mr Fayle took the stairs to the basement,
but the kids took the lift. They were allowed to
if Rubi was with them.

When the lift doors closed, Dennis turned
to Rubi. 'Where did you put the switch to
launch Prankmageddon?' he asked.

'The main switch is in your locker,' said Rubi.
'But I've installed an emergency trigger in the
clock on the front of the school. If you can't get
to your locker, use your pea-shooter to shoot it.'

'My pea-shooter?' said Dennis. 'I don't have it. It smells of fish, after I cod-liver-oiled the mayor!'

'Don't worry,' said Rubi. 'if everything goes to plan, you won't need it.'

'Hang on,' said Minnie. 'What's Prankmageddon?'

The lift doors pinged open before she could be told. Mr Fayle was waiting for them, surrounded by stacks of cardboard boxes.

'About time too,' he said. 'These are your new School Academic Diaries. I want you to count them, then give one to every pupil.'

'What?' said Minnie. 'It'll take all day!'

'Then get on with it!' said Fayle. He walked out of the door and closed it after him. They heard the lock turn, and they were alone.

Dennis had been made to keep a diary once, and he'd been surprised how much he liked to record the cool stuff he'd been doing. But why would anyone want a School Diary? That's the last thing you'd want to be reminded of! Maybe you could keep cool homework excuses in it.

Minnie ripped one of the boxes open.

'These are big enough to last a lifetime,' she said, dismayed. 'But they're for one term only!'

School **A**cademic **D**iary

SINGLE-TERM HOMEWORK PLAN

Name...................
Class...................
Teacher...................

If found please return to Mrs Clamp for reward*

*The Pupil who Lost it will clean your loo for 3 years
with their tongue

Mrs Clamp and Mr Fayle were planning 24-7 homework. There would be no spare time for sleeping, eating, hobbies, fun or mischief. Maybe that was the whole point.

The mayor's plan was going to ruin their lives.

'We can't hand these out,' said JJ. 'Look what they're called – School Academic Diaries. **SAD** for short. And if we deliver them, we'll be the **SAD** Squad! Everyone will HATE us!'

Mandi frowned. This was too much, even for kids who enjoyed schoolwork. She knew working non-stop squeezed the fun out of life, like a horrid bore constrictor...

'Fayle somehow knows we were behind the pranks,' she cried. 'It's going to take us all day just to count these!'

Minnie slapped her hand to her forehead.

'How could we be so stupid?' she groaned. 'Mandi's right. Who's going to save Bash Street School now?'

Dennis climbed a stack of boxes to test the window. There was no way to open it. He looked out and gasped. Pie Face and Mandi scrambled up after him.

The Academy bus was back, and Fayle was hurrying Academy pupils into the school.

'What are THEY doing here?' said Pie Face.

'They're taking our places,' said Mandi, 'Look, they're going towards Class 3C.'

'Those goons CRUSH inspections,'

groaned Dennis. 'Bash Street won't fail, it'll get an A plus!'

Dennis banged on the window. Mr Fayle looked over, and saw their faces peering out.

He raised a hand to his forehead, his thumb and forefinger at right angles.

'What's he doing?' said Pie Face, puzzled.

'He's giving us the 'L', calling us losers,' Mandi said. 'Only he's a teacher trying too hard to be cool, so he's accidentally doing it backwards. He's a Grade A Clown!'

'Look,' called Minnie. She was standing by the broken trapdoor Fayle had fallen into.

'Why didn't they just cover it?' said Rubi.

'They must be too used to students following the rules,' said Minnie.

'It looks like our only way out of here,' said Dennis.

'It's too dangerous,' said Mandi. 'You don't know what's down there.'

YOU DON'T KNOW WHAT'S DOWN THERE EITHER – IT COULD BE AWESOME!

I'D TURN BACK IF I WERE YOU!

STRICTLY PROHIBITED

TEACHERS ONLY

DANGER!!!

Just then, the basement door opened, and Mr Fayle saw them peering down the hole.

STOP RIGHT THERE, YOU HORRIBLE LITTLE WORMS!

Dennis looked back at the hole. *Maybe he could lure Fayle away?* he thought. *Then his pals could escape and save the school!*

If he'd thought twice, he would have realised Fayle might NOT follow him, which would leave his friends trapped in the basement while he was trapped in the hole. But Dennis never thought twice about anything.

He dropped into the hole without hesitating and disappeared. Gnasher yelped and jumped into the darkness after him.

Dennis's plan failed. Fayle didn't follow him.

'Stay where you are,' said Mr Fayle to the other kids.

Mandi looked at him, then looked into the hole. What was the worst that could happen? She had no idea – she'd never made a flow chart on what to do when a cyborg teacher locks you in the basement.

'Wait up, Dennis,' she cried. 'You'll need my torch!'

And Mandi leapt into the hole too.

Fayle rushed to the hole to stop her, but tripped on the barbed wire and fell, hard.

He lay unconscious across the hole, blocking it completely. Minnie and Pie Face tried to pull him out of the way, but he was too heavy.

'Come on!' said Minnie, heading to the door. 'We can escape before he wakes up!'

Pie Face hesitated. 'What about Dennis and Mandi?'

'They will know what to do,' said Minnie. 'Let's go!'

Chapter Eleven

THE TERRIBLE TEACHER TRAP!

Meanwhile, down in the hole, Mandi and Dennis were discovering amazing things.

'Wowser! Caves!' breathed Mandi, shining her torch around. 'This is so cool!'

She was feeling stressed and knew turning negatives into positives helped her to feel better. 'I can see dinosaur bones in the walls,' she exclaimed.

Something was blocking the hole they'd jumped down, so they had to find another way out. Dennis knew Mandi would be worried.

Mandi had the torch so she led the way.

There were arrows chalked on the walls of the tunnel. Teachers must have used these tunnels a long time ago. They hurried on and came to a dark pool of water. Mandi stopped. The water seemed to be boiling . . . no, moving.

'Oh no,' said Mandi. 'The water's full of rats!'

'No rats down here,' Dennis replied.
'The crocodiles probably ate them all.'

'CROCODILES?!' cried Mandi.

'LOOK!' said Dennis, pointing. He was right . . . some of the crocs looked angry. Some of them looked hungry. Mandi made a mental note to make a flow chart to see which was more dangerous – a hungry croc or an angry croc.

LOVELY TO HAVE SOME UNEXPECTED VISITORS FOR "LUNCH" . . .

What if the croc is hungry and angry? – Ed

On the far side of the pool, they could just make out a doorway. It was the only way out, but it was below the level of the water. It was impossible to get there.

'Urgh!' squeaked Mandi, pointing at a gargoyle carved into the wall above them. 'What's that?'

The gargoyle's tongue hung down from its mouth. Gnasher leapt up to gnash it. When he did, the tongue moved down, there was a gurgle and the water level dropped a little. Gnasher dangled there, slightly confused.

Hmmm... he looks familiar...

'Hang on, Gnasher!' said Mandi, and pulled on one of his back legs. Again a gurgle, and the water level dropped further. Dennis grabbed Gnasher's other back leg and pulled too.

Gneasy does it!

EVERY TIME GNASHER LEAPS, HE LETS ONE GO! IT'S LIKE WHEN MY DAD DOES DIY!

GO ON, GNASHER!

You're only tongue once!

As they pulled, a giant sink plug attached to a rusty chain emerged from the water and the water drained away. The crocodiles vanished down the plughole, and a dripping, wooden bridge leading to the sunken doorway appeared.

SPLOOSH!

OMG! Where does that door lead? This is exciting, isn't it?!

'Come on, let's get out of here before the crocs return,' said Mandi, as she ran across the bridge.

Things might be getting messy in the basement, but above, the inspection was going swimmingly.

Mrs Clamp had shown Mr Testy the trophy cabinet, which she had newly filled with trophies from local charity shops.

'We encourage our pupils to be the best they can be,' she said, wiping a fake tear from her eye.

Mr Testy smiled and ticked a box on his clipboard.

Then Mrs Clamp took him to visit Class

3C, which had been filled with students from Beanotown Academy. Mr Testy had been nervous about meeting the class behind the frogspawn incident, but they were very quiet and hardly even looked up. They seemed very subdued.

'Mr Fayle has really helped 3C to improve,' Mrs Clamp said. 'He finds kindness works the best.'

'Will Mr Fayle be joining us?' asked Mr Testy, ticking another box. 'He seems like a very nice man.'

'Why don't we go to my office and wait for him?' said Mrs Clamp, giving him her sweetest fake smile. 'I'm nice too, you know.'

Chapter Twelve

BENEATH BASH STREET

Dennis and Mandi high-fived as they reached the far end of the bridge. They ignored the warning sign above the door.

> ## PUPILS WHO DISOBEY WILL MEET A STICKY END!

Mandi's torch picked out a hole in the floor. They couldn't walk around it, but the gap was an easy jump. Mandi raced ahead, but something nagged at Dennis. If this place was made by teachers, why would they make it easy?

When Mandi landed on the far side, Dennis saw the rock she landed on start to sink. There was a hiss, a click and then a loud grinding noise.

HISSS... CLICK... GRIND!

Dennis quickly jumped across, then turned to catch Gnasher in his arms.

Suddenly, they felt as if they were growing taller. Or was the ceiling coming down to crush them? It was!

They looked up and saw the word HOMEWORK, carved in huge letters in the ceiling.

'Death by homework!' gasped Mandi. 'Let's get out of here!'

'I can't move my feet,' said Dennis. The floor was covered in sticky pink goop. They were stuck!

'It's bubblegum!' cried Mandi. 'Tonnes and tonnes of sticky old bubblegum!'

'What now?' said Dennis. 'We can't be crushed! We've got to save the school!'

There were two comfy chairs in Mrs Clamp's office.

'Mr Fayle won't be long,' she said to Mr Testy. 'Let's have a seat.'

And they did. *PHWWAAARPPP!!!*

Mrs Clamp squealed and jumped off her chair.

Mr Testy stood up hastily and covered his bottom with his clipboard.

THAT WASN'T ME, BTW!

IT WASN'T ME, EITHER! I HAVE A RARE CONDITION THAT RENDERS ME UNABLE TO FART. HARD TO BELIEVE, BUT TRUE!

Mrs Clamp picked up a rubber bag with an odd nozzle in it from her chair. She'd never seen one of these before.

'Ho-ho!' laughed Mr Testy. 'It's a whoopee cushion. A harmless prank!'

Academy pupils were too scared to bring whoopee cushions to school.

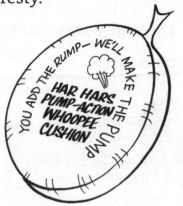

YOU ADD THE RUMP – WE'LL MAKE THE PUMP

HAR HARS PUMP-ACTION WHOOPEE CUSHION

'Hmm,' said Mrs Clamp, suddenly feeling very nervous indeed. 'Why don't I show you the swimming pool? Mr Fayle and I cleaned it ourselves . . .'

When they were gone, loud snorts of muffled laughter came from under the desk.

JJ and Pie Face crawled out.

'Did you see her face?'
said JJ, through tears
of laughter. 'I thought
she was going to die of
embarrassment!'

'I know,' giggled
Pie Face. 'They're going to see
the pool now. I wonder if Rubi
got there in time?'

WHAT'S THAT, PAUL,
MY POTATO FRIEND?

YOU'RE RIGHT. IT WOULDN'T
BE LIKE RUBI TO BE LATE...

Chapter Thirteen

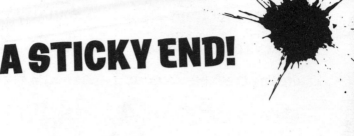

A STICKY END!

'I guess this bubblegum trap is the Sticky End,' said Dennis.

People are smart in lots of different ways. Luckily for Dennis, Mandi was an expert at solving problems.

'Dennis!' she said. 'Tell me again. What's so special about Gnasher?'

'Huh?' Dennis said. 'Well, his coat is stronger than barbed wire, he's really loyal and his teeth can gnash concrete.'

'That's what I thought!' said Mandi.

She pointed at the roof. 'Gnash it, boy!'

Gnasher leapt at the roof, and used his teeth to rip through it like it was an old cream cracker. Soon he'd gnashed a big hole in it.

The ceiling got lower and lower, until . . .

Dust filled the air, but they were alive. They quickly passed through the hole Gnasher had made in the ceiling.

BOOM!

'**WOW!**' said Dennis. 'This time the dog really did eat the homework!'

He gave Gnasher a hug.

If your feet smell like this, see a doctor – Grossed-out Ed.

'Leave your shoes,' said Mandi. 'They're well stuck.' They undid them and carried on.

'Come on,' said Mandi. 'We must be getting close now!'

Mrs Clamp led Mr Testy to the swimming pool.

'We think it's important that exercise is fun,' she explained.

'Absolutely,' said the inspector, ticking another box. 'But why is it red?'

Mrs Clamp was puzzled. 'Why is what red?'

'The water in the pool,' said the inspector.

Mrs Clamp couldn't believe her eyes. Her pool (every tile of which had actually been cleaned by pupils with toothbrushes), was indeed red. It looked like a scene from:

SHARK ATTACK 7:
The Swimming Lesson.

'I don't know!' she confessed.

Mr Testy stretched out his foot and tapped the surface of the pool. There was no splash. Just a wobble. He extended his foot even more.

WIBBLE!

'Careful, Mr Testy!' said Mrs Clamp, taking his arm.

Mr Testy tapped his foot harder, and he fell over into the pool, taking Mrs Clamp with him. He performed a perfect dad-splits as one foot slid across the pool. Mrs Clamp was dragged out onto the 'water' behind him.

Mr Testy licked the wobbly surface. 'Strawberry jelly,' he laughed.

'Why is this happening?' Mrs Clamp wailed.

Mr Testy crawled to the edge of the pool, climbed out and helped Mrs Clamp do the same.

'Another prank,' he said, giggling. 'You have a lively bunch of pranksters at this school, Mrs Clamp. Well done for encouraging their creativity and sense of fun!'

'Well, we try,' said Mrs Clamp, and they left.

Rubi appeared from the showers at the far end of the room,

'That was beautiful,' she said to herself, laughing. 'The inspector actually enjoyed it! I wonder if Minnie's got the next prank ready?'

Then she stopped laughing. 'And I wonder how Dennis and Mandi are doing?'

Meanwhile, down in the basement, Dennis and Mandi had just arrived at an ancient stone door. Above it was carved a strange word:

CONFISCATORIUM

'This must be where teachers store all the toys and pranks that are confiscated,' said Mandi.

Dennis pushed. The door creaked and swung open.

CREAK!

The Confiscatorium was full of student possessions that get taken away from pupils. Some of them were so old Dennis didn't even recognise them. But the strangest things in the room were a Viking boy and his dog. Not dead ones, but real, and alive! And they were obviously distant ancestors of Dennis and Gnasher!

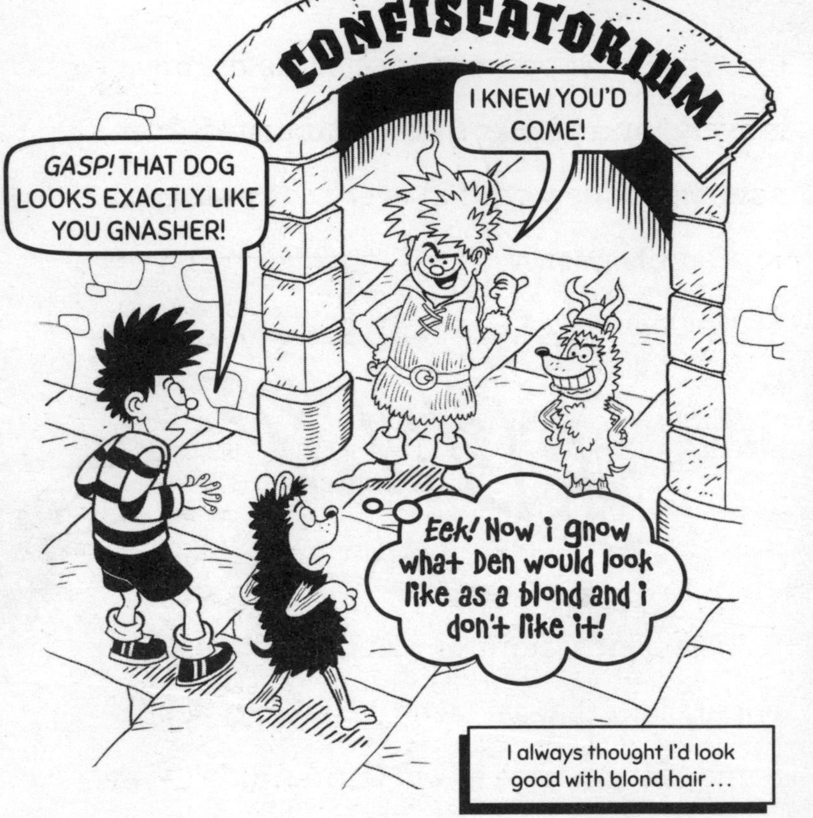
CONFISCATORIUM
GASP! THAT DOG LOOKS EXACTLY LIKE YOU GNASHER!
I KNEW YOU'D COME!
Eek! Now i gnow what Den would look like as a blond and i don't like it!
I always thought I'd look good with blond hair . . .
. . . well any hair, really!

'How?' spluttered Mandi. 'Why? When? And just O.M.G!'

'We've been waiting years for you to show up!' Viking Dennis said to Dennis. 'My teacher put a curse on us many centuries ago, keeping us here forever. All we have to keep us occupied is every toy and prank ever confiscated. Even now, we get new stuff in every day or two.'

'Thousands of toys and pranks and no one to play with,' sighed Viking Dennis. 'There has never been a tougher punishment.'

'Sounds like your teacher was an ancestor of our own Mr Fayle,' said Mandi.

Dennis turned to Viking Dennis. 'You can't just leave?'

'The curse is eternal,' said Viking Dennis. 'If we leave, we crumble to dust. Itching powder, in fact.'

'Anyway,' he added, with a sneaky wink, 'a next-gen console was chucked down here last week, so we won't get bored for about a decade.'

'Luckily,' he continued, 'you can escape to carry on our proud pranking tradition. Our school life was harsh, but yours is even harsher. Eventually, there will be no school that is ever less than 100% fun! That is our battle, my friends.'

'Before you can leave, you must prove your worth. One of these catapults is the Catapult of Ages. Pick wisely, for if you choose badly, you must remain here . . . **FOREVER!** And there's only one game controller.'

Lying before Dennis were three very different catapults. His mind raced.

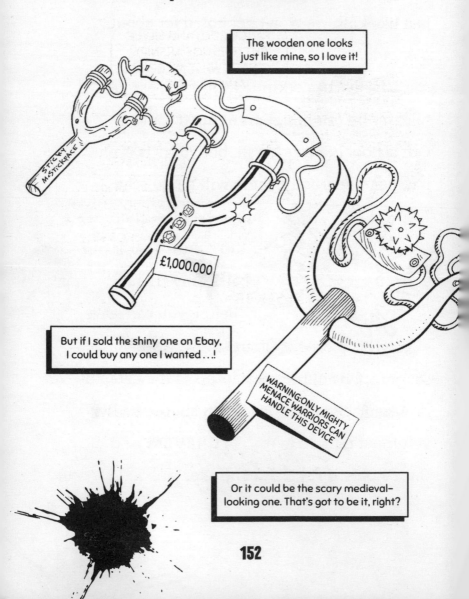

'Choose carefully, Dennis,' said Mandi. 'The Catapult of Ages will be honest and truthful – just like kids.'

Dennis picked up the plain wooden catapult. Mandi held her breath.

Viking Dennis smiled. 'You chose wisely.'

They were free to go and save Bash Street, powered by the greatest catapult in history!

'So where's the exit for kids who aren't eternally cursed?' asked Dennis, sensitively.

Viking Dennis nodded at a pool of bubbling black liquid in the corner.

'Don't worry,' he said, filling a horn with the liquid and drinking it down. 'It's fizzy cola!'

Viking Dennis handed them cool viking helmets to wear. 'Safety first.'

Dennis and Viking Dennis high-fived. Gnasher and Viking Gnasher exchanged friendly butt-sniffs.

Or was it the other way round?

Mandi thought Viking Dennis's hands looked a bit grubby, and she honestly felt dogs' bottoms were best avoided, so she settled for a friendly wave.

They stepped into the pool of cola. Mandi looked at the roof above them. There was a hole in the rock which went a long, long way up.

She heard a whooshing sound from the tunnel they'd just come through. She looked at Dennis.

'**FAYLE**,' said Dennis, nodding. 'He must be following us – at rocket speed.'

Viking Dennis took a tube of confiscated chewy mints from under his helmet, flipped the lot into the pool of cola and took a step back.

the mints aren't fizzing yet – I'm making these bubbles! snee-hee!

THESE PRANK SUPPLIES WILL COME IN HANDY!

We all know what happens when you put chewy mints in fizzy cola, right? – Ed.

'Good luck,' he said.

Nothing happened.

And then . . .

Chapter Fourteen

MR TESTY'S VERDICT

Mr Testy LOVES this horrid school, thought Mrs Clamp as she and the inspector hurried back to the lobby. He was so keen to file his report, she could hardly keep up with him!

Mr Testy had ticked all but one of the boxes on his inspection sheet. She was crushing it!

'I've seen enough,' Mr Testy said. 'This school is one of the kindest, most patient, happiest schools I've ever inspected. And do you know what I love most?'

'The curtains?' she ventured.

She realised that he loved all the things that she hated about this strange school. Creativity. Individuality. **EVEN FUN!**

'I love the way your pupils have so much fun,' he enthused. 'I've never known a school where the staff and pupils have such a good laugh together!'

'I must get back to my office and write up my report,' he said, 'so I'll get out of your . . .'

Just as he started to say 'hair', he and Mrs Clamp slipped and landed on their tummies. With legs and arms flailing, they slithered at top speed straight towards the trophy cabinet.

Minnie watched from behind Mrs Yodel's cheese plant, her hand clamped over her mouth, so she couldn't be heard laughing.

Mr Testy and Mrs Clamp dragged themselves from the pile of broken wood and bent silver that had been the trophy cabinet. The 1942 Tiddlywinks Trophy was crushed. The 1951 Crossword World Cup was smashed. The Best Linesman of 1966 Award was in pieces.

Miss Mistry's Maths

If two grown-ups are travelling at an average speed of 34mph, what noise do they make when they collide with the school trophy cabinet?

KERWHISHHH-PLANG-KLUNK-BOOF-TING-TING-GROAN!

'Gosh!' said Mr Testy. 'I'm so sorry. You must have been very proud of . . .' He picked up a flattened silver cup and read the plaque. '. . . the Deodorant Salesman of the Year for 1973?'

Mr Testy wiped his finger on the floor. 'This floor is incredibly slippery!'

His sharp eyes spotted an empty tin of Mr SuperShine Floor Polish in the bin in the corner.

'Another of your little scamps,' he chortled, 'has polished this floor so hard it's like an ice rink! You can practically see your face in it!'

Minnie held her breath. This was the moment when Mr Testy was supposed to tell Mrs Clamp that Bash Street was the worst school ever.

But Mr Testy didn't. Instead he said, 'Bash Street School has never been so good. It's my favourite school of all time. Congratulations, Mrs Clamp.'

He ticked the final box on his sheet, and wrote A+ at the bottom.

'I'm very pleased with how this inspection has gone. Mr Stamp said this was the worst school he had ever visited, but I've found the opposite. Turning the entire pool into a solid jelly is such a

SCHOOL INSPECTION
ACTUAL TEACHERS ☑
ACTUAL CHILDREN ☑
CLEAN ☑
SAFE ☑
FUN ☑

A+

creative use of maths and problem-solving skills! You must be very proud of your pupils.'

Rubi, JJ and Pie Face sneaked behind the cheese plant. Minnie signalled to them to be quiet.

'So,' whispered JJ. 'How did we do?'

Minnie made a thumbs-down signal. 'It didn't work.'

The Mistry Mob had failed.

Chapter Fifteen

FAYLE'S FINAL FLIGHT!

Mr Testy and Mrs Clamp walked out of the school, then stopped. There was an odd, gurgling sound coming from a manhole in the playground.

The manhole cover shot into the air on a geyser of what looked like fizzy cola!

Peering up, Mr Testy was astounded to see a boy, a girl and a funny little dog lifted into the air by the geyser, then dropped to the ground.

Good job they were wearing those funny helmets, thought Mr Testy.

'Hello there,' he said, when the kids had made sure all their limbs were still attached. 'And who are you?'

'Just . . . er, our **Sewer Exploration Society** in action,' said Mrs Clamp, quickly. She took Mr Testy's arm and led him towards his car. 'They're very keen.'

The rest of the Mistry Mob rushed out of the school doors.

'Do it now, Dennis!' cried Minnie.

'Or Mrs Clamp and Fayle will prevail!' added Pie Face.

'The emergency switch, Dennis!' shouted Rubi, pointing at the clock over the school entrance. 'Unleash Prankmageddon!'

Dennis pulled the Catapult of Ages from his pocket. It felt good. He dug a single cod liver oil capsule from his other pocket.

This is it, Dennis, he thought.

But he hesitated . . .

'Don't think, Dennis,' said Mandi. 'You don't need a flow chart to figure out the worst that can happen now!'

Dennis took aim and let fly. The little golden capsule arrowed through the air, hitting the centre of the clock.

SPROING! The clock face opened, and a torrent of lumpy yellow goop poured into the playground.

A tidal wave of runny, sunny liquid swept Mrs Clamp and Mr Testy off their feet. As they lay in the sticky yellow mess, the Mistry Mob gathered around. **GLOOP!**

'Are you the inspector?' asked Dennis.

Mr Testy stuck his finger in the yellow goop and tasted it.

'Custard!' he cried. 'And it's lumpy. Just how I like it!'

'I'm Dennis,' said Dennis, 'These are my friends from Class 3C.'

I'm gnot! thought Gnasher.

'Mr Fayle locked us in the basement,' Dennis continued, 'so we wouldn't be around for your inspection. He replaced us with kids from Beanotown Academy. They've been trained to pass school inspections.'

'Ridiculous,' Mrs Clamp said. 'That bump on the head has affected the boy's mind!'

'If you don't believe me,' said Dennis, 'ask Miss Mistry. They sacked her because she didn't think like them.'

'She understands that school should be fun,' Mandi added. 'She's a Bash Street kid.'

'Have you ever heard such a tall tale?' spluttered Mrs Clamp. 'Mr Fayle is far too lovely and dedicated to ever do such a . . .'

'I'VE GOT YOU NOW, YOU HORRIBLE URCHINS!'

Fayle shouted, blasting through the manhole. **'GET BACK TO THE BASEMENT BEFORE YOU RUIN THE INSPECTION!'**

SMASH!

'MR FAYLE, NO!' cried Mrs Clamp.

Fayle shut off his jets – which was unfortunate, as he was still twelve feet in the air.

'Mr Testy! I didn't see you there,' he stammered as he fell to the ground.

'Can I have a word with you in private?'
Mr Testy said to Mrs Clamp. She nodded
glumly, and led him back into the school.
Mr Fayle followed, miserably.

'I'd also like to speak to Miss Mistry,' said
Mr Testy. 'She sounds interesting . . .'

. . . and they all
lived happily ever
after. THE END

Just kidding! It's
not the end yet . . .

Chapter Sixteen

PRANK YOU, AND GOODNIGHT!

The Mistry Mob were left alone in the playground.

'What happened to you two?' said Minnie, to Mandi and Dennis.

'We had an amazing adventure under the school,' said Mandi.

'Fayle was out cold over the hole,' Minnie said. 'We couldn't move him to let you out.'

'All our pranks were awesome!' said Pie Face. 'They worked brilliantly, but Mr Testy

172

loved them – he gave us an A+!'

'That's why we still needed Prankmageddon,' said JJ. 'If you hadn't nailed that shot, the inspector would have left and we'd have lost.'

'Did we win, then?' asked Pie Face.

'I don't know,' said Dennis. 'I thought there'd be fireworks or something if we won.'

'We should get back to class,' said Rubi. 'We need to kick those snotty Academy kids out of our school!'

o PHUT!

An hour later, the Academy kids had been chased out of Class 3C and Bash Street School. The bell rang three times. Then . . .

DENNIS, JEM, PETER, MANDI, RUBI AND MINNIE SHOULD REPORT IMMEDIATELY TO THE HEAD TEACHER'S OFFICE!

'You can all blame me for this, if you like,' said Dennis, as they went down in the lift.

'No way,' said Minnie. 'The Mistry Mob sticks together, remember?'

When they got to Mrs Clamp's office, Dennis paused then knocked.

But it wasn't Mrs Clamp who opened opened the door. It was Miss Mistry. She told them Mr Testy had torn up his original report and written a new one. It still gave the school its best score ever, but Mrs Clamp and Mr Fayle got an F minus (and three poo emojis). 💩💩💩

Mayor Brown had sent Mrs Clamp and Mr Fayle back to Beanotown Academy in disgrace. Mr Belcher had discovered he actually loved to dance the tango and he'd decided that he wanted to retire after all. Mrs Creecher, a formidable ex-girl guide from East Kilbride would be taking over.

'What about you, Miss?' asked Mandi.

Miss Mistry smiled. 'I got my job back. And I've been asked to make sure Bash Street School is always a fun place for creative, curious and energetic kids. Bash Street kids, like you . . . and me!'

'Does that mean no homework ever again?' asked Dennis, eagerly.

'Don't push your luck,' said Miss Mistry.

The rest of the day was a blur. When the bell rang at 3.15, Class 3C got up to leave.

'Hang on, class,' Miss Mistry said. 'I want you all to come back tonight after dinner, please!

I've organised a special event.'

Dennis groaned. **What now?**

Miss Mistry had organised a celebration bonfire! There were fireworks and a barbecue. Walter was in charge of cooking the food, so he wasn't very happy.

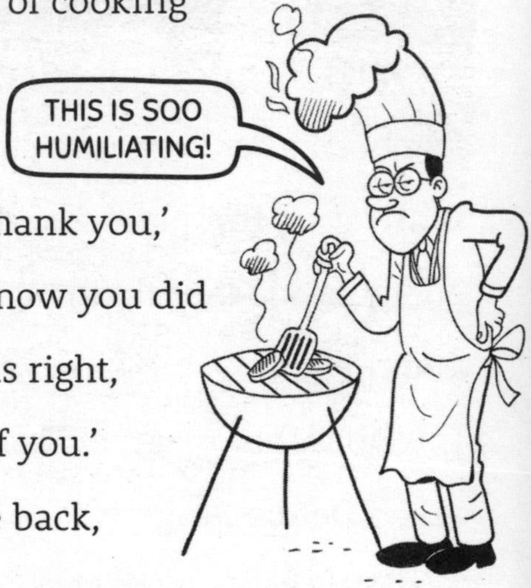
THIS IS SOO HUMILIATING!

'I wanted to say thank you,' Miss Mistry said. 'I know you did what you thought was right, and I'm very proud of you.'

'We're glad you're back, Miss,' said Mandi.

'Are you sure you can't go easy on the homework, just for a week or two?' asked Dennis hopefully.

Miss Mistry laughed. 'Speaking of

homework, check out what that lovely bonfire
is made from.'

There was a big stack of boxes by the fire,
which the janitor and Winston were emptying
into the flames. The Mistry Mob grinned.

'Best use of a homework diary . . . ever!' said Dennis. 'Clamp and Fayle did not prevail,' said Rubi, happily.

'And we all stuck together,' added Mandi.

'Anyone fancy a game of Super Epic Turbo Cricket?' asked Minnie. 'I brought my taser . . .'

THE END

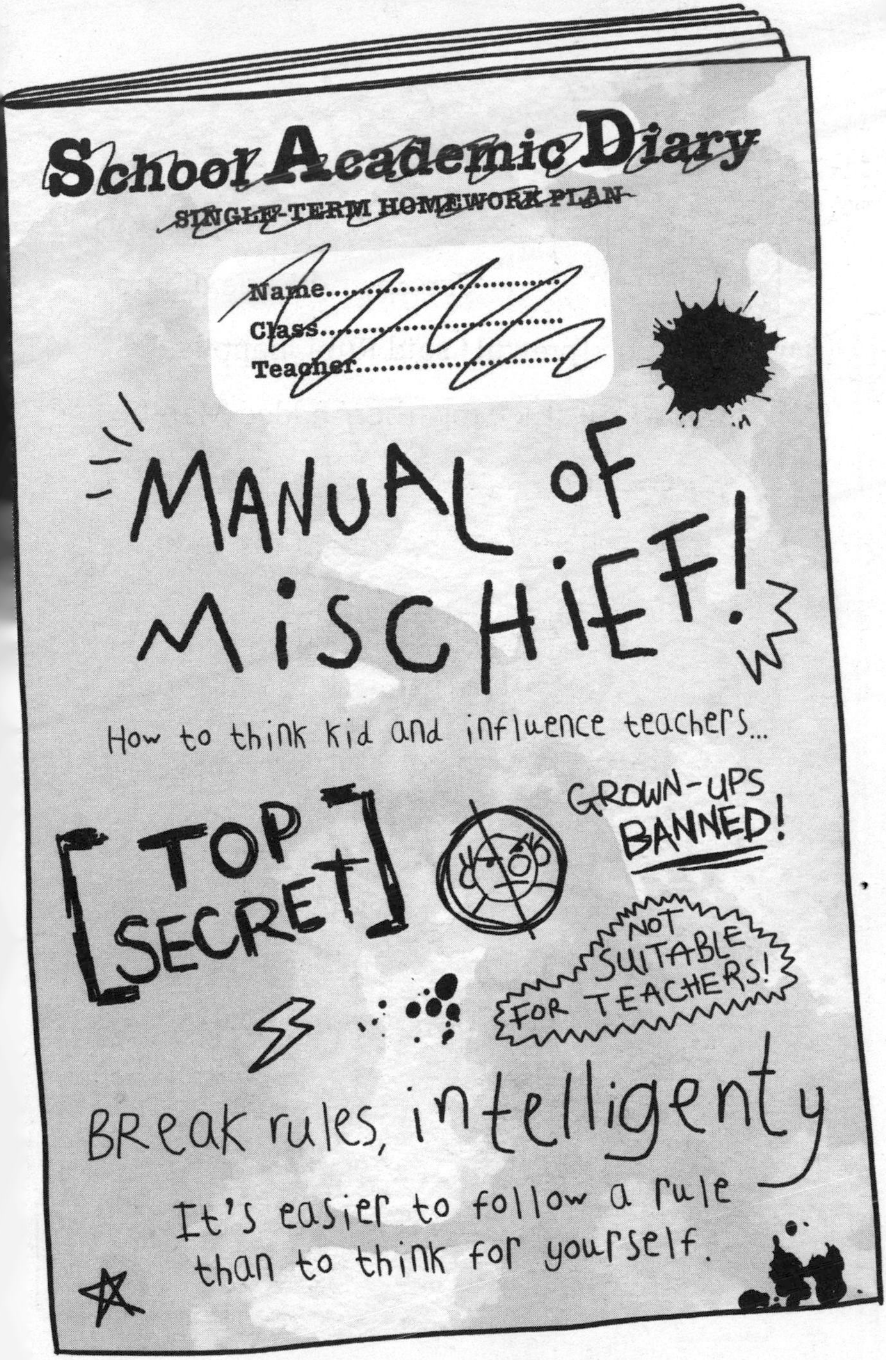
School Academic Diary
SINGLE-TERM HOMEWORK PLAN
Name..............................
Class..............................
Teacher..............................
MANUAL OF MISCHIEF!
How to think kid and influence teachers...
TOP SECRET
GROWN-UPS BANNED!
NOT SUITABLE FOR TEACHERS!
Break rules, intelligenty
It's easier to follow a rule than to think for yourself.

HIDE THIS BOOK!

This secret stash of must-know tricks, designed to help kids win life at school is a high-priority target for teachers, everywhere.

TEACHERS TALK!

BLAH

BLAH

If one gets hold of this they'll share this, quicker than you can say: "whose turn is it to bring the biscuits?!"

YOU'VE discovered the ultimate guide to leaving YOUR school feeling loads smarter than the teachers who taught you.

We, the current pupils of Bash Street School, Beanotown promise to solemnly share the tips and tricks that have made us playground legends, worldwide.

Bash St Seal of approval (so you know it's) legit!)

Take what you need, then pass it on... but kids only, O.k.? We've hidden this inside a book so grown-ups will never suspect a thing!

Some things you may hear in the background right about now...

Ooh! Look how cute, they're reading a real book!

Are you feeling OK?! It looks suspiciously like you're reading a book?

The batteries must be dead on their console

LOL!! They don't realise that as soon as kids can read there is nothing that can stop us becoming smarter than the average Prime Minister or President*

*though, that's not very hard!!

KID KNOWLEDGE IS POWER!

The secret is to NEVER grow-up.
It's a trap!

signed

DENNIS + GNASHER!

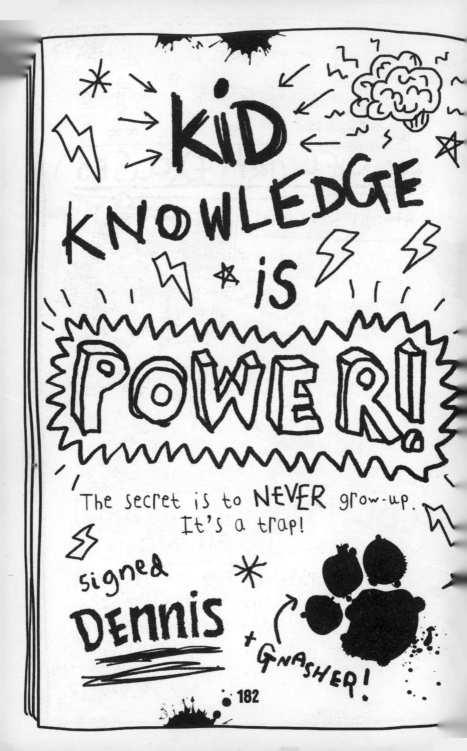

SECRET (shhh!)
LESSON 1:

HOMEWORK EXCUSES

Always have one!

This term's faves:

1. My dog ate it!

An old classic that seems to work well if you have a dog that looks like Gnasher. After all, who'd look inside him to check?!

2. My sister/brother/gran ate it!

Slightly harder to swallow (for all of them, probably). Works better if you have a very young brother or sister, or a scary looking, Gran.

183

P.T.O for more →

3. my parents wanted it framed!

If your teacher looks doubtful, say they can come for tea to view it. They'll never risk that, just in case your dog, or gran, tries to eat 'em!

4. I wanted to wait until tomorrow, until I was older + wiser... Like YOU!

Adding the final part is the clincher...unless your teacher doesn't like being described as 'older'.

Some kids swap in 'MATURE', which gives sneaky teachers the chance to ask, 'Like a cheese?'

5. I didn't want to add to your workload!

What can they say to <u>that</u>?!

LESSON 2:
ALL-PURPOSE EXCUSES

⚡ use in case of emergency! ⚡

These will buy you time to think up a smarter response...

it was... a mistake

use puppy-dog eyes!

Covers everything and would melt the heart of an abominable snow-teacher

they made me do it!

Remember to blame it on aliens, if your teacher asks, "Who did?"

About the Authors

Craig Graham and Mike Stirling were both born in Kirkcaldy, Fife, in the same vintage year when Dennis first became the cover star of Beano. Ever since, they've been training to become the Brains Behind Beano Books (which is mostly making cool stuff for kids from words and funny pictures). They've both been Beano Editors, but now Craig is Managing Editor and Mike is Editorial Director (ooh, fancy!) at Beano Studios. In the evenings they work for I.P. Daley at her Boomix factory, where Craig fetches coffee and doughnuts, and Mike hoses down her personal bathroom once an hour (at least). It's the ultimate Beano mission!

Craig lives in Fife with his wife Laura and amazing kids Daisy and Jude. He studied English so this book is smarter than it looks (just like him). Craig is partially sighted, so he bumps into things quite a lot. He couldn't be happier, although fewer bruises would be a bonus.

Mike is an International Ambassador for Dundee (where Beano started!) and he lives in Carnoustie, famous for its legendary golf course. Mike has only ever played crazy golf. At home, Mike and his wife Sam relax by untangling the hair of their adorable kids, Jessie and Elliott.